Finn and the Feline Frenemy

🐾 Read all the books in the 🐾
Life in the Doghouse series!

Elmer and the Talent Show

Moose and the Smelly Sneakers

Millie, Daisy, and the Scary Storm

Finn and the Feline Frenemy

LIFE IN THE DOGHOUSE

Finn and the Feline Frenemy

● DANNY ROBERTSHAW & RON DANTA ●

Written by Crystal Velasquez • Illustrated by Laura Catrinella

ALADDIN New York London Toronto Sydney New Delhi

ALADDIN

An imprint of Simon & Schuster Children's Publishing Division

1230 Avenue of the Americas, New York, New York 10020

First Aladdin paperback edition February 2023

Text copyright © 2023 by Danny Robertshaw and Ron Danta

Illustrations copyright © 2023 by Laura Catrinella

Photographs on pages 131, 134, and 136 courtesy of Danny & Ron's Rescue

Also available in an Aladdin hardcover edition.

All rights reserved, including the right of reproduction in whole or in part in any form.

ALADDIN and related logo are registered trademarks of Simon & Schuster, Inc.

For information about special discounts for bulk purchases, please contact Simon & Schuster Special Sales at 1-866-506-1949 or business@simonandschuster.com.

The Simon & Schuster Speakers Bureau can bring authors to your live event. For more information or to book an event contact the Simon & Schuster Speakers Bureau at 1-866-248-3049 or visit our website at www.simonspeakers.com.

Designed by Tiara Iandiorio

The illustrations for this book were rendered digitally.

The text of this book was set in Museo Slab.

Manufactured in the United States of America 1222 OFF

10 9 8 7 6 5 4 3 2 1

Library of Congress Cataloging-in-Publication Data

Names: Velasquez, Crystal, author. | Robertshaw, Danny, author. | Danta, Ron, author. | Catrinella, Laura, illustrator.

Title: Finn and the feline frenemy / Danny Robertshaw & Ron Danta ; written by Crystal Velasquez ; illustrated by Laura Catrinella.

Description: First Aladdin paperback edition. | New York : Aladdin, 2023. |

Series: Life in the doghouse | Audience: Ages 7 to 10. | Summary: Finn, a redbone hound mix with three legs, adjusts to life with his new family—and new cat sibling.

Identifiers: LCCN 2022034460 (print) | LCCN 2022034461 (ebook) |

ISBN 9781534482715 (pbk) | ISBN 9781534482708 (hc) | ISBN 9781534482722 (ebook)

Subjects: CYAC: Dogs—Fiction. | Dog adoption—Fiction. | Cats—Fiction. | Animals with disabilities—Fiction.

Classification: LCC PZ7.V4877 Fi 2023 (print) | LCC PZ7.V4877 (ebook) | DDC [Fic]—dc23

LC record available at https://lccn.loc.gov/2022034460

LC ebook record available at https://lccn.loc.gov/2022034461

To Christy Edens and everyone that works at

Danny & Ron's Rescue for their endless dedication

to all of the dogs and their fellow team members.

We love you all.

Chapter 1

FINN COULDN'T BELIEVE his luck.

First he had been taken in by two of the best humans he'd ever met: Danny Robertshaw and Ron Danta, the owners of the dog rescue where he'd lived until that morning. Then he'd been adopted by the best family ever: José and Christina Figueroa, and their nine-year-old daughter, Alyssa, who gave the best ear scratches. Now all his favorite people were in his new home, having lunch together, and that was the best too.

Danny and Ron didn't usually come along with the dogs when new families took them home. But this time José and Christina had insisted. They said something about a "feast," and that made Danny and Ron smile and hop into their car, following the Figueroas back to their house. Finn hadn't been sure what "feast" meant then, but now he did: Food. Lots and lots of food.

Danny pushed back from the dining-room table and let out a deep breath. "That was delicious!" he said.

"I agree," Ron added, setting his fork down onto his now-empty plate. "I still say you didn't have to go to all this trouble just for us."

He gestured around the table at the serving bowls and trays that remained half filled with homemade dishes: corn masa patties stuffed with cheese, avocado salad, fried plantains, yellow rice with vegetables mixed in, and a giant pitcher of iced tea. Finn knew better than to beg for scraps of people food, especially when he'd eaten already, but it all smelled so good. He kept his eyes peeled just in case some fell onto the floor by accident.

José shook his head, his shoulder-length black hair swaying as he smiled. "Please," he said, his dark eyes filled with warmth. "It was our pleasure."

Christina leaned back and cradled her swollen belly in her hands. She was a little more than eight months pregnant. Her round baby bump had grown quickly since they'd first come to Danny & Ron's Rescue to begin their search for a dog to join their family. She pushed her loose hair away from her rosy face so that the golden waves looped behind her ear and settled near her rounded chin.

"Especially for the two of you." She beamed at Danny and then Ron. "We wanted to adopt a dog as soon as possible so that he'd be all settled in before Brendan here arrived, and you found us the perfect one just in time."

She gazed at Finn then, and the reddish-brown redbone hound mix returned her smile with a happy thump of his whiplike tail on the carpet, a shake of his long, floppy ears,

and a goofy grin that left his tongue hanging

out of his mouth.

"Who's a good boy, Finn?" she cooed.

Finn barked, "Me!" and everyone at the table

laughed.

Danny nodded. "He is a special dog. We

were so happy to see how quickly he bounced back after his surgery. He will still need plenty of help getting used to having only three legs, though. Are you sure you'll have the time to work with him? I know you must be very busy preparing for the baby's arrival."

"We're sure," Christina said. "Now that school is out for the summer, all three of us will be home to help Finn adjust to his new life. Instead of teaching kindergarteners the alphabet, we'll teach Finn that three legs can be just as good as four."

José added, "We're aware that Finn will have some challenges, but we saw Rusty through them after we adopted him, and we'll do the same for Finn."

Christina reached out and held José's left

hand and Alyssa's right. "Between the three of us, by the time I give birth to Brendan, Finn will be ready to help us look after our new bundle of joy."

"Speaking of Brendan," said José, "all I have left to do now is finish getting his room set up."

"Oh," said Ron. "Is that why those boxes are in the hallway?"

José nodded. "We're converting Alyssa's old playroom into the nursery. I didn't realize just how much stuff she had in there! It's taking forever to clear it all out."

Alyssa eyed her father hopefully. "You don't *have* to," she said, twisting a strand of her long brown hair around her finger. "My room could stay just the way it is."

Her father regarded her with a knowing

look. "And where would we put the baby's crib and changing table?"

Alyssa shrugged and looked away, the corners of her lips turned down in a slight frown.

Christina tsked and said, "Now, Alyssa. We've talked about this. The baby needs a room, just like you did when you were a baby. And you've still got your own bedroom."

"I guess," Alyssa said, crossing her arms.

"Why don't you go ahead and take your dishes into the kitchen?" José told his daughter.

"Okay, Dad," said Alyssa in a quiet voice. She pushed her chair back with a squeak. She picked up her plate and drinking glass, then walked into the kitchen, a pout still on her face.

As soon as she was gone, Christina leaned toward Ron and said, "You'll have to excuse her. Alyssa is thrilled about the new dog, but she's not as thrilled about the new baby just yet. She's been the only child for nine years, and all that is about to change. Her little brother is going to kind of take over our lives for a while."

"I understand what that's like," said Ron. "Just look at us." He gestured toward Danny. "We lost a lot more than one room when we converted our house into a dog rescue. The dogs have taken over our lives too, but we wouldn't have it any other way."

Danny chuckled. "And neither would the dogs! It's their house now. We're just lucky they let us live there."

After José and Christina cleared the rest of the dishes from the table, the whole family joined Danny and Ron in the living room as they prepared to leave.

Ron bent over to scratch Finn behind his ear. He had been curled up on the rug, but now he sat up and licked Ron's hand. "I think you're going to be very happy here," Ron said, kissing the top of Finn's snout.

"I'll make sure of it!" Alyssa chirped, kneeling beside Finn to give him a quick hug.

Finn didn't know what she had said, but he definitely understood hugs and kisses and big smiles. Alyssa beamed at him now, her hazel eyes twinkling. *I bet she's fun to run and play with*, he thought, wagging his tail. Before he'd gotten hit by a car, and before his last owners had tried and failed to fix his broken leg on their own, he used to run so fast, no one could catch him. But then he'd had to get surgery, and his leg could not be saved. Since being taken in by Danny and Ron, he'd spent a lot of time lying down. At first whenever he'd tried to stand up, his back leg shook and he was unsteady on his paws. He had come a long way since then, thanks to Danny and Ron and the whole staff at the rescue. But it still might be a while before he could run like he used to, he realized. He believed in himself, though. He vowed to do whatever it took to get back up on his paws.

Danny cuddled him one last time and said, "Goodbye, Finn. Good luck in your new home." Then he and Ron walked to the door.

"Thanks again for coming," José said, shaking Ron's hand.

"Thank you for having us, and for the feast!" Ron answered. "Remember, if you need any help with Finn, we're only a phone call away."

As Finn watched Danny and Ron leave through the screen door, he whined a little. He would miss them, and all the dogs at the rescue. But then Alyssa clapped her hands together and gazed up at her parents.

"Can I give Finn the tour now? Pleeease?"

José grinned. "Of course, sweetie. Just take it slow, okay? And make sure you're there when he meets Rusty. Finn has been around cats at the rescue, and Ron said he likes them a lot, so it would be safe for us to introduce him to our cat. But it might be a different story for Rusty. He's never had to share his space with a dog before, at least not for very long; he may not be too friendly at first."

"Don't worry, Dad," she said. "Rusty's going to love Finn as much as I do!" She turned toward Finn and gently helped him to a standing position. "Come on, boy. I'll show you your new home!"

Staying close to Alyssa's side, Finn followed her through the house while she chattered on about each room and what they did there.

"And this is the kitchen, where all the good smells happen, well, except for the garbage, but you'll probably like that smell too. Oh! And here is the dining room. I sometimes do my homework here, but mostly we eat. Back there is the washing machine. When we're washing clothes you might hear a sound like 'chugga chugga chugga.'" Alyssa stopped and did a silly dance, twisting her hips left and right and pumping her fists. It made Finn like her even more. He hopped on his front paws and added some "ruff ruff"s to her "chugga chugga"s.

Alyssa laughed and waved him onward. "Nice moves, Finn! Now let's keep the tour going."

She had a happy skip to her step that almost matched Finn's uneven walk. That is, until she reached the half-empty playroom. Inside Finn could see boxes of crayons and markers on a round yellow table. Attached to the wall were shelves stacked with board games, stuffed animals, and cars made out of Lego pieces. The boxes stacked neatly in the hallway were filled to the brim with toys and jump ropes and video games.

"This *was* my playroom," Alyssa said. "But I guess it's Brendan's now."

She sighed and hurried past the room as if just looking at it made her sad. As they continued the tour past the bathroom, though, Finn caught a whiff of something that distracted him. The bathroom had a litter box in it. There was a cat somewhere, but he hadn't seen it yet. There had been a few cats at the rescue, and even though they were a little bit afraid of all the noisy dogs, they got along with Finn. He hoped this cat would be no different.

"And now I'll show you my room," Alyssa announced.

She led Finn to a long staircase. On one side was a polished wood banister. On the other was a wall decorated with portraits of the family. Alyssa started up the steps, but Finn stayed right where he was. He used to love climbing things—stairs, benches, rocks, anything really. But now he wasn't sure he could do it. He sat back on his haunches and let out a high-pitched whine. *How embarrassing!* he thought.

Alyssa turned around and covered her mouth with her hand.

"Oh, Finn, I'm so sorry. I forgot! Stairs might be a little too much for you right now. Here, let me help you."

Careful not to hurt his back leg, Alyssa lifted Finn into her arms and carried him up the stairs. When she got to the top landing, she gently set Finn back down. That's when he noticed the cat smell was stronger here than it had been anywhere else in the house. It seemed to be coming from the tall structure in front of him that looked kind of like a tree covered in soft gray carpeting. It was next to the window in a small sitting area, and had a few flat surfaces staggered on either side of the main pole. Finn could see an orange striped tail bathed in light at the very top of the pole, flicking lazily in the sun.

"There you are, Rusty," called Alyssa. "Why don't you come down here and meet your new best friend?"

A pair of amber eyes peeked over the edge of the platform, and a set of whiskers twitched under a pale pink nose. Rusty stretched and made his way down the cat tree, one level at a time, until he reached the bottom and stood

facing Finn and Alyssa. That's when Finn noticed that even though Rusty was a cat and he was a dog, and Rusty was small while Finn was big, they had one very important thing in common: they both had three legs!

Chapter 2

FINN COULDN'T BELIEVE his luck again!

Since his surgery he'd started to think he was the only animal around who'd lost a leg. But here was another one, right in his own home! He was so excited, he galloped clumsily toward Rusty. He couldn't wait to sniff the cat, lick his ear, and jump around him in a circle.

"Hi!" he barked happily, while he sniffed

Rusty's tail and paws. "I'm Finn. I live here now. How long have you lived here? Have you had three legs the whole time? How did you get up to the top of that thing? Was it hard? Could you teach me? And—"

Finn had a million more questions, but they were all cut off when Rusty let out a loud hiss and turned away.

"Ugh," Rusty said. "I don't like dog slobber! And you ask too many questions. Get lost!"

Finn whimpered in disappointment as Rusty climbed back up the cat tree until all Finn could see was his orange tail waving over the edge.

Alyssa sighed, gazing up at the cat. "Rusty, you're being rude!" Then she looked down at Finn and shrugged. "Sorry about that, buddy.

I should've warned you. Rusty takes a while to warm up to new friends. But don't worry. He'll come around!" She reached out to pat Finn's head. "Anyway, the tour's not over. Come on! I'll show you my bedroom now."

She trotted off toward a room at the end of the hall. Finn followed her in, and suddenly it was as if he were underwater. Tropical fish and dolphins and even a happy-looking octopus swam along the aquamarine walls. The theme continued onto Alyssa's bedspread, which was covered in starfish. She pointed to the octopus.

"I painted this one, and Dad painted the dolphin. We did the whole room together. He knows how much I love swimming and animals, so we made it look like the ocean. Isn't it great?"

Finn wagged his tail happily, liking the cheerful singsong of Alyssa's voice.

"I knew you would like it!" she said.

Then she moved past a storage chest to a large crate with a plaid bedsheet draped over the top. Alyssa swung open the door.

"Here's where you'll sleep, Finn. You'll stay close to me so I can keep an eye on you for a while."

Finn crept forward slowly, sniffing at the

crate. It reminded him of the ones at Danny &
Ron's Rescue, but this one had been filled with
special Figueroa touches. Inside the crate were
soft blankets and a few stuffed sea creatures
like the ones on Alyssa's wall. It all looked so
cozy and comfortable. But the smell of Rusty
was strong here too. Had he taken Rusty's spot?

Just then José knocked on the open door
of the room and peeked his head in. "Hey, I
wanted to see how the tour is going."

"I think he liked it!" Alyssa chirped. "Well,
except for the stairs . . . and Rusty. I don't think
Rusty was too happy to meet him."

José winced and swiped his fingers
through his jet-black hair. "Yeah, I was afraid
that might happen. Rusty will have to get used
to having a dog around." José came farther

into the room and grinned at Finn and his daughter. Then his eyes shifted to the right of the crate, where a cat bed sat in the corner. He lifted it with one hand and said, "Until that happens, it's probably best that Rusty sleep somewhere else for now."

"Are you sure?" Alyssa asked, looking troubled. "Rusty always sleeps here with me. I don't want him to think I kicked him out."

"He won't," José assured her. "We all have to adjust for the new arrivals, right? That includes Rusty."

Alyssa nodded, even though she seemed unsure. "I guess so."

But that night, as Finn snuggled into his new crate with Alyssa sleeping peacefully in the bed beside him, he could hear Rusty meowing loudly from outside the bedroom door. He didn't sound happy at all about not being invited in. He didn't stop yowling until Christina came to scoop him up, saying, "Come on, Rusty. Leave Alyssa and Finn alone.

You'll see them in the morning."

As Christina carried Rusty away, Finn could hear him grumbling about this being *his* room, not some drooly dog's. Finn sighed. All he could do was hope that tomorrow would be better.

Chapter 3

EARLY THE NEXT morning, Alyssa woke up at the same time as the sun.

"Good morning, boy!" she said, opening the squeaky crate door and sticking her hand in to pet a still-yawning Finn. "Ready to go for a walk?"

Finn loved the word *walk*. It was one of his favorites! He quickly shook off his drowsiness and leaped to his paws. Well, he almost did. But sometimes he forgot that without one of his back legs, his balance was different now. He teetered over onto his side, grateful for all the soft blankets around him that cushioned his fall.

"Whoa, boy, take it easy," said Alyssa. She helped him up and led him out of the crate.

Finn lowered his head. He didn't like how awkward he felt walking around now. Would he even be able to go on a walk?

Seeming to pick up on his nervousness, Alyssa knelt in front of him, gazing right into Finn's big brown eyes with her hazel ones. "Don't worry. Mom and Dad already told me you aren't ready for long walks yet, so we'll take short walks until you get a little stronger, okay?" She reached out to pat his back leg.

Finn loved her patient tone and the smell of minty toothpaste on her breath. He lunged forward and covered her face with kisses, making her giggle.

Quick as a flash, Alyssa changed out of her pajamas and threw on some clothes. Then she helped Finn down the stairs. Christina and José were already in the kitchen, preparing breakfast.

"You're up early," Christina said, greeting Alyssa with a kiss on her cheek and bending over as far as her baby bump would allow to stroke Finn's head.

"I'm taking Finn for a walk," answered Alyssa.

"Remember . . . ," José began.

"I know, I know," Alyssa cut in. "Just to the corner and back."

José nodded. "And you know how to put on the harness?"

"I think so." Alyssa retrieved the harness from a hook by the door. It was a special one made of heavy-duty nylon, with straps on the sides in case she needed to lift Finn during the walk, or if his weak leg needed a break. Alyssa placed the harness on the floor and let Finn walk into the openings for his front legs. Then she pulled it up and fastened the straps so that they didn't rub against the area where his back leg used to be. Finally, she attached the leash to the top of the harness.

"Perfect!" said Christina.

"Thanks!" Alyssa smiled as she walked Finn

to the door. "I watched a video online about how to do it."

Before they could get any farther, Rusty yowled, "Where are you going? This is our morning cuddle time!"

Alyssa stopped in her tracks and scratched behind Rusty's ear and under his chin until his chest rumbled with a deep purr. Finn shifted impatiently from one paw to another. *Morning cuddle time?* he thought. *Can't that wait until we get back?* If he didn't know any better, Finn would think Rusty was just trying to keep Alyssa from spending any more time with him.

"Sorry, Rusty. I guess I forgot to say hi to you this morning," Alyssa said.

"I think he wants to go too." José grinned as he prepared bowls of fruit.

Alyssa shook her head and nuzzled the tabby. "I can't take you with us on our walk. But we'll be right back, okay?"

Rusty doubled up on the purring and made his eyes big and sad, as if he might never be happy again.

"Nice try, Rusty," Alyssa said. "That look doesn't work when you're begging for more treats, either." Then she patted her pockets. "Oh no. Treats! I almost forgot to bring some with me. Hold on, Finn!"

With that, she rushed off to the pantry, where they kept the dog treats.

The moment Alyssa was out of sight, Rusty's eyes narrowed and he glared at Finn. "Oh, you just think you're *so* smooth, don't you?" he meowed.

"Me?" Finn was confused. He looked down at himself. "Do you mean my hair? Thank you for noticing! The groomers had to give me a bath and brush it for an extra long time yesterday morning, but it looks smooth? Good. I was worried that—"

"Don't pretend you don't know what I'm talking about," Rusty interrupted. "Everyone

thinks you're *so* cute, with your wet nose and your waggy tail, but I see right through you. All you want is to steal Alyssa's attention away from me. Well, enjoy it while you can, buddy, because I've got news for you: I'm a cat. We *invented* being cute! And in no time at all, I'll steal her attention right back and be Alyssa's favorite pet in the house. Then you'll be the one sleeping in the living room, not me."

Finn huffed, getting angry himself now. He understood Rusty needing time to get used to a dog in his space. But Finn wouldn't stand for any cat accusing him of something he didn't do. Or didn't mean to do, anyway.

"You've got it all wrong," he insisted. "I don't want to steal anybody. I just want to be friends."

Rusty narrowed his eyes again and licked one raised paw. "Yeah, right. I'm onto you, dog."

Before Finn could say anything else, Alyssa came back, waving a small bag of treats. "Got 'em!" she called. She tucked the bag into her pocket, then picked up the end of Finn's leash. "Okay, let's go!"

Finn followed her out the door, but he kept one eye on Rusty the whole time. Once they got outside, he could see the tabby sitting in the windowsill, watching them sullenly.

Just as Alyssa had promised, their walk was short and slow. Finn liked the way Alyssa took small steps, encouraging him all the while. She still walked a little faster than him, but she would say, "Good boy!" and slip him a treat whenever he caught up. By the time they got back to the house, Finn felt a lot less wobbly as he walked. But all that hard work made him think about food.

When Alyssa heard Finn's stomach rumble, she said, "Sounds like someone's ready to eat. Let's get you and Rusty some breakfast!"

"Here," said her father as she entered the kitchen, handing her two bowls set into a raised plastic rack. "Don't forget to use these. That way he won't have to bend too far down to eat. We don't want him to put any extra stress on his shoulders."

"I know, Dad," said Alyssa. "They're just like the ones we got for Rusty."

Finn watched Alyssa's every move as she scooped out some kibble from a large container and poured it into one bowl, then filled the other with water. But she didn't put them down until she had filled Rusty's with his soft cat food too. Finally, she placed the two sets of bowls onto the floor, side by side.

"Are you sure that's a good idea?" her mother asked as she cut into her waffle. "Putting their bowls so close together?"

Alyssa shrugged. "Maybe if they eat together, they'll become friends. It worked for Dereeka and me when we met in the school cafeteria." She settled at the dining-room table in front of her own breakfast, but she didn't eat. She was too busy staring at Finn and Rusty, her eyes filled with hope.

Finn didn't bother listening for any words he knew. He just stuck his snout into his bowl and started scarfing up his breakfast. Rusty did the same without looking Finn's way at all. For a while, the only sounds in the kitchen were Finn's satisfied grunts and chomps, and Rusty's delicate munches. To Finn, this felt just like mealtime at the rescue, when he'd been surrounded by dogs who were all his friends. *Is that what Rusty is becoming?* he wondered. *Are we friends now?* But halfway through his meal, Finn lifted his head to take a breath. That's when the fishy smell of Rusty's food hit his nose. Finn sniffed the air and then lowered his snout into Rusty's bowl.

"Hey!" yowled Rusty. "Stick to your own food!"

"Friends share," Finn said matter-of-factly. "But what are you eating? It smells different from mine."

"Of course it does," Rusty purred. "It's like I said—I'm a cat, so I get the tastiest food. Mine is way better than yours."

Finn snorted. "That isn't true. My food is delicious too!"

"Doubt it," said Rusty with a twitch of his whiskers. "Dog food is the stuff they decided wasn't good enough for cats."

"Is not," said Finn.

"Is too," Rusty replied calmly.

"Is not!"

"Is too."

They went back and forth like that for a while, until José said, "Maybe we ought to separate them. Sounds like they're getting on each other's nerves."

Alyssa held him off. "Wait, Dad. Maybe they can work it out."

After another round of *is not, is too*, Finn said, "I'll prove it. Let's switch bowls. You can taste mine, and I'll taste yours."

"No way," Rusty objected. "I don't want any of your—"

But Finn had already grabbed the edge of Rusty's bowl with his mouth. He figured he would move Rusty's bowl in front of him, and nudge his own bowl in front of Rusty. Then they could really see whose food was best. Rusty did not like that plan, not one bit.

"You're slobbering all over my breakfast!" Rusty yowled.

Alyssa sounded upset too. "Stop it, Finn!"

Finn would have listened, but it was too

late. When he tried to turn toward Alyssa, the paw at the end of his wobbly back leg skidded on the smooth linoleum floor, throwing him off-balance. "Uh-oh." He fell backward, and Rusty's bowl went flying. It seemed to move in slow motion as it arced up toward the ceiling then flipped upside down in midair. Suddenly, it was raining cat food—and most of it landed right on Rusty's head with a splat.

Oh no! Finn thought. He hadn't meant to do that. In fact, he couldn't have pulled it off again if he'd tried. It had all been a terrible accident. But he knew Rusty wouldn't think so.

"Here, let me help clean you off," said Finn. He rushed to Rusty's side and lapped at the cat food still clinging to Rusty's fur. *It's tuna!* Finn thought as he licked. That was the fishy smell,

and it was no better or worse than his food.

"Blegh! Stop slobbering on me already!" Rusty hissed, backing away. "I can clean myself, thank you very much. And I'll do a better job than you ever could."

"I'm really sorry, Rusty," Finn said. "It was an accident. I was only trying to—"

"That was no accident. You did it on purpose!" Rusty hissed furiously. He started to walk toward Finn with his tail sticking straight up and his back arched.

Finn scooted away in fear, but Alyssa got between the two of them. "Stop it!" She shooed the cat in the other direction, saying, "You need a time-out, Rusty! Go clean yourself up and calm down. I'll check on you later." She pointed out of the room with a stern look. Rusty glowered at Finn one last time before disappearing down the hall.

Then Alyssa turned to face Finn, who bowed his head and lifted his eyes up at her. It was the only way he knew to tell her he was sorry. Alyssa understood. "I know that was an accident," she told Finn. "But you've got to give

Rusty a little space, or you'll never get along!"

Alyssa stroked Finn's clean coat then and told him everything would be okay, but Finn could tell from Alyssa's knitted eyebrows that he had messed up big-time. *Great*, thought Finn. It was bad enough he didn't have full control over his own leg, but he'd put that frown on Alyssa's face, and he now had to live with a cat who couldn't stand the sight of him. Instead of friends, they were becoming frenemies.

Chapter 4

OVER THE NEXT few rainy days, Finn gave Rusty all the space he could—which meant he didn't give Alyssa any space at all. He followed her everywhere—to the kitchen to watch her make a sandwich, to the living room to watch her read a book on the couch, and even to the bathroom to watch her brush her teeth. He became her little shadow.

So he was right by her side when she knocked on the door of her old playroom. After a moment, José opened the door a crack so that all Finn could see was a sliver of his face.

"Can I help you?" he asked.

"I was thinking maybe *I* could help *you*," answered Alyssa. "You're painting in there today, right?"

"Yes."

"I'm good at that. Just give me a brush, and—"

"I'm sorry, Peanut. I don't think that's a good idea," José said. "If you come in, Finn will want to come in too, and all these paint fumes would bother him."

"But Mom can watch Finn for a little while," Alyssa pleaded. "I'm always your little helper.

We had so much fun painting my bedroom, remember?"

"I know, sweetie," José said. "But . . . okay, the truth is, I don't want you to see it until it's done. So today, you can help me by making sure Finn doesn't come in here and touch the wet paint or anything. The last thing we need is to have dog prints all over the house to clean up. I've got to get the room ready in time for Brendan, right? He could come any day now!"

Alyssa sighed. "Okay. I'll find something else to do with Finn, then."

"That's my girl. Thanks, Alyssa!"

With that, José closed the door. Finn gazed up at Alyssa, who looked back at him and sighed again. "Let's see if it's still raining."

Finn followed Alyssa to the living room,

where she went to the window and looked out. Finn watched as Alyssa went from dull and disappointed to bright and bouncy.

"Finn! The rain stopped, and it looks sunny and warm outside! Do you know what this means?"

Finn's tail wagged quickly from left to right. He didn't know why Alyssa was so excited, but all of a sudden, he was too. He barked and pawed at her sneaker.

"It means I can finally show you the surprise I have for you!"

Finn panted now, letting out a few more energetic yips. Alyssa's happy vibe was contagious.

"What's that?" she said, cupping her ear. Her thin eyebrows raised as if she was really trying to understand Finn's barks. "What's the surprise? Well, I'm not just going to tell you. That wouldn't be any fun. But I think you're going to love it!"

She hurried up to her room then, leaving Finn at the foot of the stairs. At the top of the landing, Finn saw Rusty lounging near the banister, his tail waving in the air like a flag. He seemed to be smiling. "Looks like Alyssa's running away from you," he said.

Finn huffed. "She's coming back for me. You'll see."

But part of him worried that Rusty was right. If he could only climb the stairs, he could find out for himself. He placed one paw on the bottom step, but the last thing he wanted to do was embarrass himself in front

of Rusty by not being able to make it to the top. Instead, he sat and waited, trying to be patient. "I don't want to go upstairs right now anyway," he reasoned.

Rusty just blinked at him slowly with what looked like a smile teasing the edge of his mouth. "Sure you don't."

Thankfully, a few seconds later, Alyssa came rushing down the steps, wearing a bathing suit with big bright flowers all over it. She was carrying two towels and some kind of vest in her hands. Rusty padded down the steps after her and observed as Alyssa fit the black-and-yellow vest around Finn's body.

"It's called a life jacket, Finn. Our veterinarian recommended it for you." She backed up to admire her handiwork. "It's perfect!"

she exclaimed. "You look like an adorable bumblebee."

"What's going on?" Rusty meowed. "Where's *my* jacket?"

Finn ignored him. He was still a little upset that Rusty had made fun of him for not being able to climb the stairs. So instead, he focused on Alyssa, who gestured for Finn to follow her outside. They cut through the kitchen, where Alyssa slid open the patio doors that led to the backyard.

As soon as Finn stepped outside, he understood why Alyssa had been so bubbly. The brown tarp that had covered a big section of the ground was gone. Now Finn could see that it had been hiding white steps leading down into sparkly blue water. They had a pool! And beside it, Christina was already lounging on a beach chair, soaking up the sun. When she saw Alyssa, she said, "Oh, is today the big day?"

"Yep!" Alyssa replied. "I'm going to give Finn his very first swimming lesson!"

"That's wonderful, Peanut," said Christina. "Dr. Breyer did say swimming is a great way to help strengthen Finn's back leg without putting too much stress on his joints. Now, you're a great swimmer, but this is new to Finn. It might be hard for him at first. So go slow."

Alyssa nodded. "I will." She put the towels down and carefully waded into the pool. When she had gone down a couple steps, she turned around and called to Finn. "Come on, boy. Don't be scared. I'm right here for you."

Finn was hesitant. Alyssa hadn't steered

him wrong yet. And the water did look inviting. But he wasn't sure what to do.

Christina hauled herself up from her chair and said, "I think he might need a little incentive to get in."

"I don't have the treats with me," Alyssa moaned.

Christina winked. "There's more than one way to a dog's heart." She walked to the plastic storage bin next to the house and pulled out what looked like a long, neon green inflatable balloon in the shape of an alligator. "Your father picked this up at the store the other day. It's a pool toy that floats. We thought it might help if Finn had something to hold on to in the water."

She tossed the alligator into the pool, and

it bobbed along the surface. Finn's eyes lit up. There was nothing he liked more than a new toy, and this one had a toothy smile and looked perfect for batting around with his paws! Screwing up his courage, Finn stepped into the pool one paw at a time. Pretty soon, he was floating in the water, but he wasn't moving. *Now what?* he thought.

"Good boy!" Alyssa cried. "Now let's try paddling with your paws."

She took each of his front paws in her hands and moved them up and down in the water, making little splashes in the pool. When Finn began to do it on his own, Alyssa clapped. "That's it! You've got it." Then she moved behind him and supported his belly with her hands. She showed him how to press his back leg against her to push himself forward while he paddled. He was confused at first and kept trying to turn around to see Alyssa. But she would keep moving forward, redirecting his attention to the alligator, which Alyssa started calling Al.

It took a long time, and it wasn't easy, but finally Finn got close enough to Al to grab him with both paws.

"Hooray!" Alyssa and Christina cheered together. Finn soaked up their big smiles. He did it!

Christina came and sat at the edge of the pool, letting her feet dangle in the water. "Good job, Peanut! If you work with him every day like that, pretty soon, he'll be able to swim the length of the pool all by himself."

For his first time, Finn thought he'd done pretty well, but all that swimming was hard work. He found he was too tired to paddle back toward the stairs, so Alyssa guided him in like a boat, with the alligator leading the way. Alyssa helped him climb out of the pool and pulled the alligator out too, laying it on the deck to dry. While she went to fetch the towels, Finn spotted Rusty sitting by the patio door. He had been watching them swim, Finn realized. All day yesterday, Rusty had ignored him altogether, even during meal times. But maybe now he was ready to start becoming friends. *Good timing!* thought Finn. *I bet he doesn't even know about the pool, but I'll show him. He's going to love the water!*

Just as he had on his first day in the house, Finn went galloping toward Rusty, full of excitement. "Hey, Rusty! Did you know we have a pool? It's full of water! It's so great. I can swim now. Alyssa taught me. Do you want to learn how to swim? Can cats swim? You just have to move your paws and kick your leg and—"

As Finn kept rambling, Rusty retreated farther and farther away, his back rising and his hair standing on end. "Stop!" he hissed. "Of course I know what a pool is, and I hate it! Water is the worst. Who would want to get soaking wet like you are? That sounds horrible!"

Finn paused, his tail drooping. "What do you mean?" he asked, genuinely confused. "Getting wet isn't so bad. To get dry, all you have to do is shake out your coat like this. Watch."

Finn shook his whole body, sort of like Alyssa had when she did the "chugga chugga chugga" dance by the washing machine. Only, when Finn did it, he sent water spraying in every direction. When he was done, he panted happily. But Rusty didn't look pleased at all. In fact, he looked angrier than Finn had ever seen him—angry and very, very wet. His usually soft orange fur was soaked through and plastered to his head.

"You did that on purpose—again!" Rusty shrieked, his claws popping out. He backed away from Finn . . . and landed right on top of the pool toy. His sharp claws sank into Al's plastic surface, and suddenly, Rusty wasn't the only one hissing. The alligator deflated, making a sad *sssss* sound as the air leaked out. Soon Al's toothy grin crumpled, and his inflated body looked more like a bright green tarp. It was an accident, but that didn't make the alligator any less flat.

"Nooo!" Finn barked. "That was my favorite toy in the whole world!"

"Oh please," said Rusty. "You say that about everything."

"That doesn't matter. It was my new favorite," insisted Finn. "Alyssa gave it to me."

Rusty tried to shake the water out of his fur. "So what? She gives me toys all the time."

Finn grumbled. Why was it always a competition with Rusty?

Christina sighed from the edge of the pool. "They're at it again," she said, shaking her head. "I'd better separate them for a while." But getting up was easier said than done. With her big belly in the way, standing up took some doing.

Alyssa waved her mom off. "It's all right. I've got it," she told her. She grabbed a towel and moved between Finn and Rusty.

"Enough, you two!" she cried. She shook her finger at the tabby. "That wasn't very nice, Rusty." She quickly dried him off the best she could with the towel then pointed to the open patio door. "Now, go inside and think about what you've done."

Rusty lifted his chin and tail and did as he was told, but just before he entered the house, he turned to give Finn a baleful look. "This isn't over. I'm going to be Alyssa's favorite pet in this house if it's the last thing I do!"

Finn was disappointed. Here he'd thought the pool would bring them together, but it had only pushed them further apart. He slumped onto the deck. At least Alyssa could see the argument had been all Rusty's fault. But then she spun around and shook her finger at him, too.

"And you," she began. "What did I say about giving Rusty a little space, hmm?" She came toward Finn, unclipped the life vest, and pulled it off. "There won't be any more swimming today," said Alyssa. "Learning to get along with Rusty is even more important than learning how to doggy paddle. You guys are family now! So you have to find a way to be friends. Until you do, it won't be much fun around here."

Finn didn't understand what Alyssa was saying, but he recognized her frown. It was the same expression Ron had the time he accidentally on purpose chewed through a pillow and got stuffing all over the floor. Rusty had gotten Finn in trouble!

At that moment, neither one of them was Alyssa's favorite pet. Finn huffed in frustration. He didn't think they had to compete for Alyssa's attention, but if that's how Rusty wanted it to be, then fine. Finn would show that surly cat he was in it to win it!

Chapter 5

THE NEXT DAY, after Finn's afternoon walk, the doorbell rang. Alyssa ran to answer it. When she opened the door, Finn saw another girl about Alyssa's age standing on the other side. She had perfectly round brown eyes, dark brown skin, and black hair pulled up into a curly pouf at the top of her head. But the very best thing about her, as far as Finn was concerned, was the stuffed hippo she had in her hands.

"Hi, Dereeka!" Alyssa called.

"Is he really here?" Dereeka asked, stepping into the living room with a big smile on her face.

"See for yourself," said Alyssa, sweeping her arm behind her. Finn, never more than a few feet away, bounded forward and sniffed Dereeka's hand, then sniffed the hippo extra hard, nibbling at its foot.

Dereeka giggled. "I

think he likes the toy I brought him." She let it go, and Finn trotted away with it dangling from his mouth.

"Every new toy is his favorite," Alyssa said with a smile.

"Well, come on, let's go play with him!" Dereeka suggested, heading toward Alyssa's playroom as they usually did.

But Alyssa stopped her. "We have to stay here," she said, looking glum. "My playroom isn't really mine anymore."

"It isn't?" Dereeka said, her eyes wide. "What happened? Did you get in trouble or something?"

Alyssa shook her head. "No, nothing like that. My parents are turning it into the baby's nursery."

"Oh!" Dereeka breathed a sigh of relief. "That makes sense. It's a bummer you're losing that room, but you must be so excited! The most adorable things ever are dogs, cats, otters, and babies. And you're about to have three out of four in one house! You're so lucky."

"I guess." Alyssa shrugged. "Babies *are* pretty cute. But lately, it seems like this one is all anybody talks about. It's *Brendan this* and *Brendan that.* . . . He's not even here yet, and he's already stolen my room. It's only a matter of time before he takes over the whole house!"

Dereeka raised one eyebrow at her and tilted her head. "Really? Won't he be about this big?" She held her hands a couple feet apart.

"Okay, fine," Alyssa said with an eye roll.

"Maybe it won't be the *whole* house. But you know what I mean. I just feel like once Brendan comes, there won't be much room for me anymore."

Her friend sat on the floor in front of Finn. While he gnawed on the hippo's snout, Dereeka tugged on its back legs, and they played tug-of-war until Finn snarled playfully and shook his head back and forth. Dereeka giggled and let go. "You win!" she said. Then she looked up at Alyssa. "At least you've got a new dog to play with."

Alyssa sat on the floor too, gazing at Finn. "That's true. Finn is the best. Even if he is a little drool machine."

Hearing his name, Finn let go of the hippo and snuggled against Alyssa's waist. He gazed up at her adoringly, and she booped him on the nose.

"Awww," Dereeka said. "Who cares if he drools a little? He's so cute!"

Alyssa smiled. "He really is."

Together, the two of them cuddled Finn and called him a good boy. He was having the time of his life. That is, until Rusty padded into the living room.

Good, thought Finn at first. *Let him see how much Alyssa loves spending time with me.*

But Rusty was not about to give up that easily. He padded over and rubbed his head against Alyssa's back, purring loudly. She hardly seemed to notice, though; she was too busy giving Finn belly rubs. Rusty tried flopping down between Alyssa and Dereeka, then rolling over to expose his own furry belly, a move that never failed to get an *Awww*. Most humans were powerless to resist an adorable cat with his paws waving in the air. But Alyssa and Dereeka just gave him a quick pat and went right back to gushing over Finn. After a while, poor Rusty had had enough.

He flipped onto his paws and stiffened his ears as he stared at Finn.

"So now you're trying to take Alyssa's friends from me too, huh?" Rusty hissed. "Well, let's see how you like it!"

Still holding Finn's gaze, Rusty snatched up the stuffed hippo in his mouth and ran.

"Hey! That's mine!" Finn barked.

He pulled himself away from Alyssa to chase after Rusty. He followed him around the

couch, under the dining-room table, and past the potted plant in the corner, nearly knocking it over with his tail. With the weight of the hippo slowing Rusty down, Finn thought he had a chance to catch up to him. But then Rusty did the unthinkable: he ran up the stairs.

Finn came to a stop at the bottom step, gazing up the long staircase, finding Rusty grinning at him from the top.

"Aw, what's the matter, Finn? A few stairs are too much for the greatest dog in the world?" His tone dripped with sarcasm.

Finn huffed. His back leg was already tired from chasing Rusty around the house. He doubted it would get him up these stairs. But he also knew he would never hear the end of it if he didn't at least try. Plus, Rusty had his hippo, and he really, really wanted it back. *You can do this!* he thought.

In his mind, he visualized himself running up the stairs as easily as if he were walking in the park. But in reality, each step was a fight. He tried to put all his weight on his two front legs so he could just lift the back one, but that got harder and harder to do as he went. And when he put weight on his back leg, he felt unsteady, as if it might give out at any moment and he'd fall down the few stairs he had managed to climb. The worst part was that Rusty lounged on the top landing, batting his hippo around, not even worried that Finn might reach him to snatch it away.

About a quarter of the distance up the stairs, Finn finally had to admit defeat. He was way too tired to keep going. He had to head back down. Once he was on the ground floor again, he looked up at Rusty and sighed. "Fine, you win today. But just you wait. I'm going to get up these stairs one day, and then you won't be able to get away so easily."

Rusty just blinked at him, unfazed. "If you say so."

"I do. And I'm going to tell Alyssa you stole

my toy. We'll see how much of a favorite pet you are then."

"Go ahead, tattletale," said Rusty, letting out a long yawn.

Finn found Alyssa and barked up a storm, but he wasn't sure she understood what he was saying.

"Maybe he wants a treat," Dereeka suggested.

Alyssa shook her head. "I think he's complaining about Rusty."

Finn moved forward and tugged on the hem of her shirt, urging her to come with him. If he could just show her how Rusty was holding his hippo hostage, he knew she would help.

"Is he trying to show you something?" Dereeka asked.

"Guess I'd better go find out." Alyssa finally got to her feet.

Finn yipped and led her to the stairs, but before he reached them, the hippo came flying down from above, plopping right in front of him. He looked up and found Rusty peering at him through the staircase railing, his amber eyes glimmering in the dim light. Finn grumbled. Rusty had clearly nudged the hippo over the edge of the landing just in time so that Alyssa would think Finn was barking for no reason. Finn had to hand it to Rusty—he was pretty smart. But he was also getting under his collar.

"Why did you do that?" Finn barked.

"Do what?" said Rusty. He blinked innocently and licked his paws. "Find your toy for you? I'm just trying to help."

"Are not!" Finn barked.

"Am too!" Rusty yowled.

José walked up behind Alyssa then. "What is all the racket about?" he asked.

Alyssa shook her head. "Finn and Rusty are arguing again. Rusty stole his toy and took it up the stairs. I think Finn tried to go after him, but he couldn't make it all the way up."

José frowned. "I was afraid of something like this. I didn't think we needed a gate to block the stairs, but maybe I should pick one up, just to make sure Finn doesn't hurt himself trying to go after Rusty."

"Not yet, okay?" Alyssa pleaded. "I don't want Finn to be afraid of the stairs or think he can't climb them just because he has three legs. He's a lot stronger than he thinks he is.

One day he'll climb those stairs without even thinking about it. I'll keep working with him."

"I don't know . . . ," said José, pinching his chin between his fingers.

"Leave it to me." Alyssa stooped to pick up the hippo and held it out to Finn, who grabbed it gently in his jaws. "All he needs is a little confidence. Then Rusty will stop messing with him, and then they'll be the bestest friends that ever were."

Dereeka cleared her throat. "Ahem."

Alyssa grinned at her. "Second bestest friends."

"All right, sweetheart. I trust you," José said, cupping Alyssa's cheek. "But if I see it getting worse between them, we might have to think about keeping them apart. For now, how about I make you and Dereeka a snack?"

While Alyssa went off with her friend to the kitchen, Finn stayed in place. He would normally be glued to Alyssa's side, but he was afraid to take his eyes off Rusty. He took up a position at the bottom of the stairs, glaring at the tabby who had gotten the better of him.

But Rusty just continued grooming himself, taking his sweet time cleaning his fur and nails. "Stare all you want," he mewed, "but you're the one who decided to compete with me. Don't get mad just because I'm winning."

"I'm not the one who made this a contest," Finn whined. "And you're not winning!"

"I am," said Rusty confidently. "And tomorrow, I'm going to prove once and for all that I'm the best pet on the block."

"What are you going to do?" Finn asked. He couldn't help being curious.

"You'll see."

Finn had no idea what Rusty had planned, but if it was any cuter than a purring cat twitching his pink nose and batting his big amber eyes, Finn was about to lose big-time.

Chapter 6

THE NEXT DAY, Finn woke up early, eager to start proving to all the Figueroas that he—not Rusty—was the best pet on the block . . . whatever that meant.

Because Alyssa had laid out her bathing suit and his life jacket already, he knew they would be having another swimming lesson after breakfast. *This time*, Finn thought, *alliga-*

*tor or no alligator, I'm going to swim like a fish
and make it all the way across the pool. Alyssa
will be so impressed, she will give me all the
treats she has, and Rusty will have to admit I'm
the favorite.*

With those happy thoughts still in his head,
he wolfed down his breakfast faster than he
ever had, and walked a little faster, too, when
Alyssa took him to the corner and back. She
even had to tug on his leash a couple of times
and tell him to slow down.

"You can't wait to get in the pool, can you?"
she asked.

Finn wagged his tail extra hard when he
heard the word "pool." Images of the clear blue
water filled his head, and he pictured paddling
through it with ease.

When they got home, Alyssa wasted no time getting into her swimsuit, putting on Finn's life vest, and leading him out to the pool. As before, she waded in first.

"Come on in, Finn!" she called when she was waist-deep in the water.

Finn turned in a circle to rev himself up, then made his way toward Alyssa. With each step he took, his stomach gurgled. But he ignored it. *I'm probably just excited,* he thought. Soon he was floating along in the water beside Alyssa. She took his paws in her hands and reminded him how to paddle and how to push out with his back leg. The gurgling in his stomach got stronger, and the way he bobbed in the water made him queasier with every splash. But still he told himself, *It's nothing.*

Alyssa backed away from him to take up a position halfway down the pool. "Swim to me, Finn. You can do it, boy!"

I can do it! Finn thought. *I can make it to Alyssa. And I don't feel like the washing machine is doing that "chugga chugga chugga" dance in my stomach. Nope, not at all.*

But the more he told himself that, and the more he bobbed and splashed in the water, the stronger the "chugga chugga" feeling got, until . . .

Blegh! Finn up*chugga*d his whole breakfast out into the pool.

"Oh no!" Alyssa cried, clearly grossed out. Her nose wrinkled as she swam toward Finn, carefully avoiding the upchucked kibble. She turned Finn around, guided him toward the steps, and called out, "Dad, come quick!"

José hurried over from his chair by the pool. "What's wrong?"

"Finn is sick. He threw up in the water," Alyssa replied.

Her father glanced over at the kibble floating on the surface and whistled. "Yeah, he's sick, all right. Swimming so soon after eating breakfast might've been too much for him. I'll take care of the pool. You go ahead and dry Finn off and take him inside. Fill his bowl with some fresh water. That ought to make him feel better."

As Alyssa removed Finn's life vest and toweled him dry, Finn realized his stomach did feel better, but his heart felt worse. He had been looking forward to showing Alyssa how well he could swim. Instead, all he'd done was make a mess.

He was still reeling from the embarrassing turn of events when Rusty came trotting into the yard. *Perfect,* thought Finn. Just when he was at his lowest point, Rusty showed up to unveil whatever it was that promised to nab him the title of favorite pet. Finn saw that he was carrying something in his mouth. Was it a toy? A stuffed animal? Finn only knew that it was small and gray with a plump little body and a long thin tail. Rusty dropped it proudly at Alyssa's feet.

"I brought you a present!" he meowed. He shot Finn a smug look. "A special gift from your favorite pet."

But the way Alyssa shrieked meant anything but *thank you*.

"Aaahh! It's a mouse!"

Alyssa leaped onto a deck chair, gripping the towel she had been using on Finn for dear life. Just then, the stunned mouse seemed to realize it had been set free. It darted toward José, who swiped at it with the net he used to clean the pool. When it spun and zipped toward Finn, he barked at the tiny gray rodent. It turned tail and headed straight for the open patio door, just as Christina was coming out.

When she saw the mouse speeding her way, Christina shrieked and stomped her feet, sending the mouse scampering toward the bushes, where it disappeared beneath the fence. After it was gone, Christina planted her hands on her hips and grinned. "Brave mouse to come into our yard with Rusty around."

"Rusty's the one who brought him here!" said Alyssa, still standing on the deck chair. She explained how Rusty had come into the yard carrying it in his mouth and how he'd dropped it at her feet.

"Awww, Rusty brought you a present," Christina said, putting her hand on her chest as if she'd never heard anything more adorable.

"What?" Alyssa yelled as Christina helped her off the chair. "Why would he think I'd want a mouse?"

"Because *he* likes mice. For him that would be a great gift."

Alyssa scrunched up her nose and glanced at her cat. "Well thanks but no thanks, Rusty!"

Finn would have gloated about Rusty's present being a giant flop, but he was still feeling queasy, like he might have some kibble left in his stomach getting ready to make a surprise appearance. Plus, he saw the disappointed look on Rusty's face. His tail had drooped and the satisfied look in his amber eyes was gone. Finn couldn't help feeling sorry for Rusty, and for himself.

Chapter 7

THAT NIGHT, FINN hid in his crate, curled up with his blankets and stuffed animals. Alyssa had brought him here to take a nap after all the excitement by the pool, but he hadn't felt much like moving since. He just couldn't get it out of his head that he had let Alyssa down.

She and her parents seemed to realize that

he needed a little alone time, but he did have one surprise visitor.

Rusty slinked into the room, jumped onto Alyssa's bed, and slumped down until his chin rested on his paw. He stared into Finn's crate, twitching his whiskers.

"What are you so down about?" he asked.

Finn shook his head as if he couldn't believe his ears. "My swimming lesson today

went terribly. I couldn't even make it halfway across the pool, and then I got sick. Alyssa will never want to swim with me again."

"So what?" Rusty said, lifting his head. "I cough up fur balls all the time. It's no big deal. I'm the one who should be upset. Did you see the way Alyssa reacted when I gave her my present? I mean, who wouldn't like a nice juicy mouse?"

If Finn had to guess, he'd say the answer was probably nine-year-old girls. But he didn't want to make Rusty feel any worse than he already did.

"You're right," Finn said. "Humans aren't always good at knowing when you're doing something nice for them. When I lived at the rescue, I always showed the humans where the stinkiest smells in the yard were by rolling around in them. But they didn't seem to like that much, either."

Rusty groaned. "Don't try to make me feel better. We both know the truth: Alyssa chose you as her favorite pet before I even gave her the mouse. I don't even get to sleep in this room anymore. It's only a matter of time before she forgets about me altogether."

Finn was shocked. He'd never heard Rusty sound less than confident. Finn had thought he was the only one who wasn't always so sure of himself. But maybe he and Rusty had more in common than having three legs.

"That isn't true at all!" he told the cat. "The only reason Alyssa spends so much time with me is because she thinks I can't take care of myself. My leg isn't getting stronger as fast as I thought it would. I couldn't have even gotten to this room without her help. I still can't climb the stairs, so she had to carry me. And that's not the worst part. . . ."

Rusty perked up his ears. "What could be worse than that?"

"I think Alyssa wants you and me to be friends, but no matter how hard I try, I can't make it happen. She probably wanted us to start getting along before the baby comes, but so far, I've failed," Finn whined, and buried his head under his blankets.

For a while, everything was quiet. Finn closed his eyes, hoping if he stayed hidden in his crate long enough, all his troubles would magically go away. But soon something even more surprising happened. He felt a soft, furry body settle down next to his and snuggle against his side. Rusty had come into his crate! And what's more, the cat who had kept his distance since Finn had arrived was now cuddling with him, and even purring.

"I'm sorry," Rusty whispered. "I guess I haven't made things too easy for you here."

Finn pulled his snout from beneath the blankets. "Well, I did dump food on your head and get pool water in your eyes."

"Yes, but I know you didn't mean to. Just like I didn't mean to pop your pool toy. Want to know the truth?" he asked.

Finn met Rusty's eyes and waited.

"Getting used to having only three legs was hard for me too."

Finn was shocked. "It was? But you're so graceful. Your balance is perfect. You can even climb to the top of that carpet tree thing in the hall!"

"It wasn't like that in the beginning. I fell all the time at first, and I couldn't jump or run like I used to." He stood up then and balanced on just his front leg and one of his back paws while he held his head up proudly and waved his tail. "But look at me now!"

Wow, thought Finn. He had to admit he was impressed. "Do you think I can get better too?"

"I know you can," answered Rusty. "Tell you what . . . maybe instead of competing against each other, we should work together. We can both be the favorite pets."

That sounded like a great plan to Finn! To show his appreciation, he licked Rusty's face from his chin to the tips of his ears. And this time Rusty let him.

Chapter 8

WHILE ALYSSA WAS off at Dereeka's house the next day, and Christina and José were working on the nursery, Rusty and Finn took advantage of having the rest of the house all to themselves. Rusty led Finn to the far wall of the living room, facing a high window with sunshine streaming through the panes.

"You see that windowsill up there?" Rusty pointed his tail at it.

Finn barked, "Yes. What about it?"

"It's my favorite place in the whole house. The sill is long enough and wide enough to stretch out on, and the sun makes it nice and warm. Plus, it's the perfect spot to spy on birds and squirrels."

That last part sounded good to Finn! Nothing better than a good squirrel sighting.

"Anyway," Rusty continued, "I couldn't jump up to the windowsill at first. My leg wasn't strong enough. But the thought of getting up there made me want to try—especially when Christina hung a plant over it that I really wanted to chew on."

"So what did you do?" Finn asked.

"I figured out that I may not have been able to jump from the floor straight to the window-sill, but I could get onto the couch cushions, then the arm of the couch, and then jump onto the windowsill." Rusty demonstrated by making all the jumps to the windowsill then coming back down the same way. He made it seem easy.

Finn was still confused, though. "What does this have to do with me climbing the stairs?"

"It's about finding different levels!" Rusty mewed. "I practiced working on shorter heights until my leg was stronger and I didn't have to do that anymore. You can do the same thing."

It all sounded so reasonable. Finn doubted it would be as easy for him, but he figured it wouldn't hurt to try. He padded forward, ready to follow the cushion-arm-windowsill path that Rusty laid out. But before Finn could make his move to the couch, Rusty blocked him.

"No, no, no! I didn't mean for you to do *exactly* what I did! The windowsill is way too small for you. You need your own goal to focus on, and the right motivation. And I know just the thing."

As Finn watched, Rusty darted out of the room and came back a few moments later carrying something familiar in his mouth—a stuffed hippo.

"Hey! That's my toy!"

Rusty laid it down in front of him, resting his paw on the hippo's nose. "Oh, this toy? You want it?"

Rusty scooted down so that his forearm

was on the floor and his butt wiggled in the air. It was his way of saying he wanted to play.

"Yes!" Finn barked. "Give me the hippo!"

Rusty seemed to wink at him. "If you want it, come and get it!" he called. Then he snatched up the toy in his jaws and took off running.

Finn chased after Rusty. But just like last time, he couldn't catch him. And just like last time, the chase ended at the stairs. Rusty stopped a few steps up and laid the hippo down beside him. "Well, there's your toy, Finn. Go ahead and take it."

Finn huffed. He tried to reach the toy from where he stood, but it was just out of reach. He had to climb up a couple stairs just to get a little closer. His leg felt wobbly as always, but he pushed past it. He had to get that hippo! But just when he finally found his snout within inches of the stuffed animal, Rusty picked it up again and climbed up a few more steps.

"Oops, you almost had it," Rusty taunted.

"Come on," Finn whined, getting frustrated. "Give it back."

"It's right here. All yours, Finn. You just have to grab it."

Again, Finn gathered up his strength and climbed a few more steps. He was just about to clamp down on the hippo's stubby tail when Rusty swooped it up first and climbed a few more levels. Finn growled. He couldn't believe Rusty was doing this. It was so mean! So immature! So . . . effective.

It kept on like that, with Finn climbing and Rusty moving the toy right before he could get to it, until finally, Finn had had enough—and so had his leg.

"I give up!" Finn announced. "You win. You can have the hippo. But you should know you're not a very good friend, and my food *does* smell better than yours, and I didn't want the hippo anyway, and, and . . ."

"Are you finished?" Rusty asked calmly.

Finn grunted to say that he was, in fact, finished.

"Good. Now turn around and look behind you."

Finn craned his head to peek behind him, and he could hardly believe his eyes. He was more than halfway up the staircase. He'd never made it that far before!

Finn looked back at Rusty, this time panting at an excited pace that almost made him dizzy. "I did it, didn't I!"

Rusty casually licked his paws. "Let's not get ahead of ourselves. You did better than last time. But you still haven't made it to the top. We're going to work on this every day until you do. Every day it will get a little easier. But in the meantime . . ." Rusty padded down the stairs to meet Finn where he was, and laid the hippo in front of his paws. "Here you go. You earned it."

Finn pounced on the soft gray creature before Rusty could change his mind. "You know, you're pretty annoying," he told the cat. "But you're kind of great, too. Is this what it's like to have a brother?"

Rusty twitched his whiskers. "As close as a

cat and a dog can get, anyway. Now hold still. You have a chunk of hair sticking up, and no brother of mine is going to be seen like that." Rusty started to groom Finn, and even though he was still a little annoyed about the game of keep-away, Finn let him.

Over the next few days, Rusty taught Finn everything he knew about getting around the house as a three-legged animal. For starters he showed him how to avoid slipping on the floors while running around. "Just stay on the area rugs and mats," Rusty advised. "That's why you slipped in the kitchen. You didn't keep your paws on the mat. Very important!" They became friendly enough to try each other's food. (Finn thought Rusty's tuna-and-veggie medley wasn't half bad, and Rusty admitted Finn's kibble was tastier than he'd thought it would be.)

But the main thing Rusty did every day without fail was steal Finn's hippo. The chase always led to the stairs, and every day Finn made it a little bit farther than he had the day before.

Finally, one sunny summer day, Rusty and Finn were playing their usual game of hippo hijinks. But this time when Rusty told Finn to turn around and see how far he'd come, Finn realized he was at the top of the stairs. He'd made it! He and Rusty celebrated with a friendly wrestling match that was more like hugging. Finn knew that it would be a while longer before he felt as comfortable on his three legs as Rusty felt on his, but thanks to his new feline friend, he was well on his way.

"Let's go get some water," Rusty suggested. "Teaching is thirsty work!"

Together they made their way back down the stairs. Finn noted that going down was much easier than going up. Especially when he saw Alyssa waiting at the foot of the stairs with a big grin on her face. Had she been watching them the whole time? Why else would she look so proud? She must have seen Rusty steal his toy over and over again, and had let them work it out for themselves. But she had never been far away.

Alyssa beamed at them both. "You're such good boys," she said, petting Finn with one hand and stroking Rusty's fur with the other.

"I'm so happy to see the two of you getting along."

Finn rolled onto his back, letting Alyssa give him a nice belly rub. Rusty got into the same position, making Alyssa giggle. "All right, Rusty," she said with a smile. "You get a belly rub too."

Finn had never heard Rusty purr quite so loudly. At that moment, he wanted to pay Rusty back for his kindness. And he thought he had the perfect idea.

Chapter 9

LATER THAT AFTERNOON, after success-
fully climbing the stairs a second time, Finn
urged Rusty to come with him to Alyssa's room.

"Is this going to take long?" Rusty asked.
"Because I had a busy day of napping planned."

"I had an idea. You remember how you
gave Alyssa that, um, present?"

Rusty's fur bristled. "I know she didn't like

the mouse. You don't have to rub it in."

"I'm not!" said Finn. "The reason it flopped is because you gave her a gift that *you* would like. But this room is filled with things *she* likes."

"Okay . . ."

"So maybe you could give her things that look like the stuff in this room," Finn continued. "Look around. What do you see?"

Rusty and Finn both gazed around Alyssa's under-the-ocean-themed room. Of course there were the sea creatures dancing on the wall, but for the first time Finn noticed that near the bottom were lots of tiny seashells and jewels spilling out of a sunken treasure chest. Over the chair by her desk Alyssa had draped her favorite bathing suit, which was covered in big yellow flowers. She had a star-shaped night-light plugged into the wall and a match-ing string of fairy lights draped above her headboard.

"She likes pretty things like flowers and seashells," said Rusty. "And shiny things like stars and lights."

"Sounds like a good place to start," said Finn. "I'll help you find some pretty, shiny things to give her, and she'll forget all about that mouse."

Together, Finn and Rusty searched the house and the yard for anything they thought would catch Alyssa's eye. Before long, they had quite the collection gathered: flower pet-als that had fallen from the hanging plants in the kitchen, shimmering rocks from the gar-den, and a fuzzy pink slipper they found under the couch. Each of them had even included a favorite toy. From Rusty it was a small plastic ball that lit up when he batted it around, and from Finn, a stuffed starfish from his crate. They placed their little mountain of treasure right in front of Alyssa's bedroom door and waited patiently.

"Do you actually think Alyssa's going to like this?" asked Rusty.

"No," answered Finn. "She's going to love it."

It wasn't long before Christina and Alyssa came looking for them.

"There you two are," said Alyssa, walking toward her room. "Didn't you hear us calling you? It's time for dinner."

"Awwww, look!" Christina said. "Rusty's collected more presents for you." She pointed to the random items piled in front of Rusty.

Alyssa kneeled down to examine them more closely. "This stuff is all for me? Are you being serious?"

"I am," said Christina. "I saw these two walking around together today, and I didn't know what they were up to until now. But this is how cats show their love sometimes."

Alyssa beamed as she touched the pink slipper and turned the colorful pebble in her hand. "I know you meant well with the mouse, Rus, but this is *so* sweet! Thank you."

She nuzzled Rusty and let him lick her cheek with his scratchy pink tongue.

"And thank you for helping him," Christina said to Finn, reaching out to cuddle him, too.

"They really are friends now, huh?" said Alyssa.

"Better than friends," said Christina. "They're like brothers. They fight sometimes and get on each other's nerves, they take each other's stuff and compete for attention, but they also play together and keep each other company. They teach each other things, and help when they can." She gazed down at her daughter. "That's how it will be for you and Brendan too."

Alyssa looked from her mother's belly back to Rusty and Finn, who were now tugging on either end of the slipper. Alyssa grinned. "Maybe that won't be so bad."

"It might be kind of great," Christina agreed. "You'll be an awesome sister. And thanks to you, these two knuckleheads will be good furry big brothers to Brendan when he comes. I just know it."

What Finn knew was that his plan had worked! Alyssa and her mom looked really happy, he and Rusty were friends, and the fuzzy pink slipper was his new favorite toy.

Chapter 10

FINN TOOK HIS time eating his breakfast the next day. And he didn't rush through his morning walk. Alyssa had laid out the life vest earlier, so he knew that he would be getting another swimming lesson today, and this time he didn't plan to blow it.

As Alyssa clicked the vest into place, she spoke softly to him. "Now, Finn, there's nothing to be nervous about. We're just going to have fun, okay?"

Finn licked her cheek and wagged his tail. He was ready.

Rusty sat near—but not too near—the edge of the pool, eying the water as if it might leap up and bite him.

"Are you going to swim today too?" Finn asked.

"Don't be ridiculous," he answered with a hiss. "I'm only here to cheer you on . . . or laugh if you belly flop."

Finn groaned. *Could* he belly flop? As confident as he had felt moments ago, now he couldn't help thinking about his last adventure in the pool. "Oh no," he said, nerves creeping up on him. "I'm not sure I can do this. . . ."

"I'm just kidding," Rusty said, placing his paw on Finn's. "You're going to do great. I still don't get why anyone would want to get in the water." The way he glared at the pool, it might as well have been filled with toxic sludge. "But if you can handle the stairs all by yourself, swimming should be no problem. You got this!"

With newfound confidence, Finn followed Alyssa into the pool, while José, Christina, and Rusty looked on.

"You can do it, little guy!" Christina called out.

"Move those paws!" added José.

To Finn's amazement, he found that Rusty was right—this time swimming felt easy! His leg had grown stronger than he realized. All those practice sessions going up and down the stairs with Rusty had really helped. He paddled easily through the water to meet Alyssa at the far end of the pool, and he didn't even get sick on the way! He swam right into Alyssa's waiting arms, and everyone cheered—even Rusty.

"Que bueno, Finn!" José said, crouching by the edge of the pool so he could pet Finn's head.

"Yes, great job, Finn! And Alyssa, you too . . . oooh!" Right in the middle, Christina's cheer had turned into a surprised gasp. She touched her belly with both hands.

"What is it?" José asked, looking concerned.

"I . . . I think the baby is coming!" she cried. Her eyes were wide with a mixture of surprise and excitement. "We need to get to the hospital."

"And we need to get out of this pool,"

Alyssa said to Finn. She turned him around so that they faced the stairs, and they swam back across the pool together. Meanwhile, José called his mother to come stay with Alyssa, Finn, and Rusty. As soon as Alyssa's grandmother, Abuela Marly, arrived, everyone rushed out onto the driveway, where José hustled Christina into the car along with an overnight bag. Before they could close the passenger-side door, Finn hopped up so his paws were on Christina's legs. She was taking long deep breaths, and her face was flushed. He barked and tried to lick her chin. He knew something was going on with Christina, and he just wanted to help.

"It's okay, boy," Christina said, kissing his snout. "I'll be all right. I'll be back soon."

But she wasn't back soon. It was two whole days later that their car rumbled into the drive- way.

"Here they come!" Abuela Marly announced as she peered through the window, her smile lighting up her whole face. "Is everyone ready?"

"Ready!" shouted Alyssa, holding up her WELCOME HOME, BRENDAN! sign. She had colored in the words with bright green marker and drew baby bottles and teddy bears beside them. Finn spun in a circle and barked, his tail wagging wildly. Rusty sat on his haunches, licking his paws. If they were about to have company, he wanted to look his best.

Finally, the door opened, and José entered first, followed by Christina, who carried a tiny bundle in her arms, no bigger than one of the stuffed animals in Finn's crate. Alyssa's new brother had arrived!

"Ay, bienvenido, mi nieto lindo," said Abuela Marly, welcoming her grandson. After José brought in their bags and took them to the room, he sat on the couch next to Christina. Finn inched forward slowly until Alyssa noticed.

"It's okay, Finn. You can come meet him," she said.

Finn got closer and sniffed the baby's delicate head, the receiving blanket he was swaddled in, and the tiny toes sticking out from the other end. Brendan smelled like baby powder and milk—his new favorite smells! Rusty jumped onto the couch and snuggled

in beside Christina. He looked at the tiny baby

laid out on Christina's lap and purred.

"These are your big brothers, Brendan—

Finn and Rusty. And this is your sister, Alyssa."

They all cooed over the adorable new

arrival until José said, "Alyssa, I think it's time

for that surprise I mentioned earlier. Let's show your brother his new room."

Everyone stood, and Alyssa took the lead with Finn right by her side. Finn thought she seemed a little nervous, but when she turned the knob and opened the door, her face lit up.

The nursery was beautiful. There was a cream-colored changing table with white dresser drawers down the side, a wood-framed crib, and a matching rocking chair across from it. But the best part was the mural painted on the mint-green walls. Christina and José sat on a park bench with Alyssa between them. In her lap with a tiny knit cap on was Brendan, looking up at Alyssa adoringly. Sitting on the grass in front of them were Finn and Rusty, each wearing collars that said BIG BROTHER on them, and the mural version of Alyssa wore a T-shirt that read BEST BIG SISTER EVER.

"Is that . . . me?" Alyssa asked with wonder in her eyes.

"The one and only," said José. "That's why I didn't want you to help me before. I would've been done sooner with your help, but I wanted you to be surprised too."

Alyssa's mouth curled into a grin. "Do you really think I'll be a good big sister?" she asked.

"Of course you will!" said her mother, laying a reassuring hand on her shoulder. "After we saw the way that you helped Finn get stronger by teaching him to swim . . ."

". . . And the way you watched over him

and Rusty to make sure they got along," José continued.

". . . And helped discipline them when they didn't, we knew you would be the best big sister Brendan could ever hope for. Just like you're the best daughter *we* could ever hope for," Christina finished.

The family hugged then, careful not to squeeze the baby still in Christina's arms, and Finn wanted in!

He stood on his back leg, pressing his paws against Alyssa's hip. "What about me?" he barked.

"And me!" Rusty yowled, rubbing his head against Alyssa's ankle.

Alyssa giggled. "Oops! Almost forgot Brendan's furry older brothers." She knelt down and snuggled them both. Alyssa sat on the floor with them, Finn settling under her arm and Rusty curling up on her lap. And as Finn watched Christina and José lay the baby in the crib to sleep, he had never felt more grateful for his new life, his three legs, and his best friend, Rusty.

Danny & Ron's Rescue is a real place in South Carolina. Both professional horse trainers, Danny Robertshaw and Ron Danta have been rescuing dogs ever since 2005, when they started helping animals in Louisiana in the wake of Hurricane Katrina. But they didn't stop there. Soon they opened their hearts and home to dogs who had suffered in puppy mills and dog fights, who had lived in shelters and junkyards, or who had been abandoned and were living on the streets. With assistance from a hardworking staff, including veterinarians and groomers, the dogs in their care are spayed or neutered, vaccinated, dewormed, groomed, and microchipped. They are one of the only organizations that does not have an adoption fee, but survives strictly on donations. But what makes Danny & Ron's Rescue truly unique is that the dogs live in their actual house and often sleep in the bed. At any time, they have as many as eighty-six dogs inside, with an additional thirty-five to forty dogs on the farm. There are so many more dogs than humans there, now, that Danny and Ron consider themselves guests in the dogs' house.

What was once a quiet home for two, including their horse stables, is now a safe haven for dogs who have been injured, abused, or neglected. There, not only do they receive organic food and a warm place to sleep, but they are loved and treated like part of the family until they are adopted by a family all their own. Since the founding of their rescue, Danny and Ron have saved more than thirteen thousand dogs.

Finn was one of those lucky dogs. Once named Huckleberry, he was found in a cardboard box near a trash can outside the CVETS, Columbia Veterinary Emergency Trauma and Specialty Clinic in South Carolina. A

receptionist at the clinic happened to be outside on her break when she noticed what
she thought was a taped-up box of garbage.
Something told her to look into it, and thank
goodness she did, because inside she found
a redbone hound mix puppy fighting for his
life. It was a hot day, and the pup was having

a hard time breathing. A *stat* emergency was called, and the CVETS team jumped right into action.

Finn's leg had been broken at least a week before, and although someone had tried their best to wrap it, it hadn't been done properly, and the leg was not healing the way it should. The veterinary technicians realized the injury was serious. Sadly, the damage was too severe and had gone on too long; his leg could not be saved. The only option left was amputation. However, a procedure like that is costly, and it can be difficult to find a home for an injured dog with special needs.

But Danny Robertshaw and Ron Danta were up for the challenge. They immediately agreed to cover Finn's medical care and find

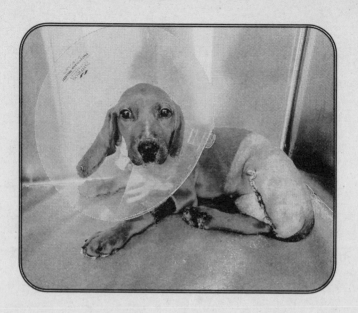

him a loving home. Only one month later, Huckleberry was adopted by Sara Tittle of Kentucky, who renamed him Finn and introduced him to his new best friend, a three-legged cat! Finn loves to run and play, and he is the handsomest hound in town.

As for the characters in this book, Alyssa, Brendan, Christina, and José are named after a real family in New York, who are friends

of the writer's and are raising two adorable dachshund pups of their own, Shea and
Roosevelt. Marly is Alyssa and Brendan's very
proud grandmother. Alyssa's friend Dereeka is
named for the writer's best friend, who has a
loveably hyper hound shepherd mix named
Dax, and whose first cat was an orange tabby,
a cool customer named Rusty.

It is thanks to heartwarming stories
like Finn's that Danny & Ron's Rescue was
highlighted in the documentary *Life in the
Doghouse*, which initially premiered on
Netflix and is now available on most major
streaming platforms. The film details how
the rescue came to be, shows the daily challenges of running the twenty-two-acre farm,
and highlights some of the special dogs that

have called it home over the years. Since its debut, *Life in the Doghouse* has won the title of Best Full-Length Documentary at the Tryon International Film Festival in 2018, and it was an official selection of the Frameline San Francisco International LGBT Film Festival, the Provincetown Film Festival, and Newport Film. It has been profiled on everything from the *CBS Evening News* to the *Today* show and the Hallmark Channel.

If you would like to find out more about Danny & Ron's Rescue and how you can help dogs like Finn, visit their website at DannyRonsRescue.org, or learn more about the documentary at LifeintheDoghouseMovie.com.

Turn the page for a sneak peek of

Millie, Daisy, and the Scary Storm!

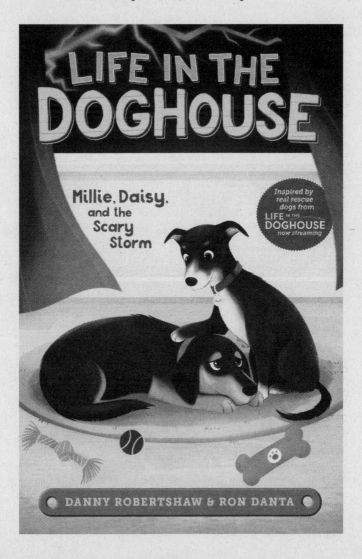

OUTSIDE THE COZY brick house that was Danny & Ron's Rescue, a storm was raging. At least that's what it sounded like to Daisy. She had hidden underneath a blanket the minute the dark clouds rolled in, and now she was too scared to do any more than peek out.

"Aw, come on, Daisy. It's not *that* bad," said Millie. "It's just a little rain. See for yourself."

"No thank you. I'm fine right here."

Millie, Daisy's best friend in the whole world, sat right by the porch door, panting happily as she looked out at the drops of water falling into the yard.

She's so brave! thought Daisy. She couldn't figure out why Millie wasn't as scared of rain-storms as she was. After all, a terrible storm had once taken away their home. Rain had fallen for days, flooding the streets of their Louisiana town. If it hadn't been for the courageous people who came by in a boat to rescue Daisy and Millie from their porch, she wasn't sure what they would have done. Eventually Danny Robertshaw and his partner, Ron Danta, took them both into their home in South Carolina. For months afterward, any time a thunderstorm came through, Daisy would run to hide under the bed, and Millie would have to find her and convince her to come out.

To help Daisy face her fears, Ron hired a special trainer—Eileen Clark. Eileen had helped figure out what triggered Daisy's fears and taught her better ways to react when she felt afraid. It had worked . . . mostly. Over time Daisy had gotten a lot better. She stopped hiding under the bed, but she still didn't like rainstorms.

She curled into a tight ball now and squeezed her eyes shut. But soon she felt a tug at the edge of her blanket. Daisy opened her eyes to find Millie gazing down at her kindly.

"I know you're scared," said Millie. "But I promise there's nothing to be afraid of. Have I ever lied to you?"

"No," Daisy said.

"That's right. And I never will. Come look at the rain with me. You might even think it's pretty if you give it a chance."

"I don't know . . . ," Daisy said timidly. "What if the storm gets worse?"

"Well, then I'll be right by your side, and we'll keep each other safe. Deal?"

Daisy thought about it for a while. She did feel safer any time Millie was around. And if her friend wanted a little company, that was the least she could do.

"Okay," she said. "But if I see one strike of lightning—"

"You can come right back here and hide under the blanket," finished Millie.

Slowly, Daisy untangled herself from the

yellow knit blanket and followed Millie to the porch door where they sat side by side, looking out at the yard. Daisy had to admit that her friend was right. It *was* kind of pretty. The rain fell gently on the grass, leaving behind little puddles that would probably be fun to splash in later. The dark clouds had thinned out, and there was a rainbow arcing across the light gray sky.

"Wow," said Daisy in surprise.

"See?" Millie wagged her tail. "I told you so."

Daisy licked Millie's ear to say thank you and then settled down on the floor beside her friend. She wasn't sure she would ever be a fan of storms, but she knew without a doubt that she trusted Millie and was glad they were here together.

"I guess there won't be any playtime in the yard today, girls," said Danny, walking up to stand behind them. "Sorry about that."

Ron was in the next room preparing medication for Cleo, the miniature schnauzer who had an ear infection, but he looked up with concern. "I hope this rain passes soon," he said.

Danny nodded. "We'll have to prepare in case it rains at the adoption event. But let's hope for the best. I would hate for anything to keep our pups from finding good homes." He reached down and stroked first Daisy's head, then Millie's. Then he went to assist Ron in the kitchen.

Even though they had a staff to help them run the rescue, Danny and Ron usually had plenty to do around the house. Before they'd started saving dogs together, only the two of them had lived there, and they'd spent most of their time training horses, teaching people how to ride the horses in competitions, or entertaining friends. But now they spent a lot more of their days cleaning out crates, ordering chew toys, and giving love and attention to all the dogs who lived in their home. There were so many, Ron joked that he and Danny were just guests in the dogs' house.

Daisy had been happy when she came to the rescue, and she thought it would always be her home. But Danny had said the word "adoption." She knew that meant a nice person or family would come to meet a dog, and if they liked each other, the dog would go home with them. Sometimes they'd come back to visit and tell the others all about their new lives. Danny and Ron loved to see how happy the dogs were in their forever homes.

Daisy was always thrilled for them too. But she liked her life just as it was. She whined softly.

"What's the matter now?" asked Millie. "I thought you'd gotten used to the rain."

"It isn't that," said Daisy. "Did you hear Danny and Ron mention an adoption event?"

Millie nodded. "They usually plan them to be part of the horse shows," she answered. "But why would that worry you?"

Daisy shot a glance behind her at Ron, who was now giving Apollo his heartworm medication. He was so loving and gentle, Apollo didn't even mind. "You don't think *we'll* get adopted, do you?"

Millie scratched behind her ear with her back paw. "Don't be silly. We're not going anywhere if we don't want to," she answered. "We'll always have a home here. Danny and Ron said so."

"But what if they changed their minds?" Daisy panted, covering her snout with her paws. "If we get adopted by different families, we might never see each other again!"

"Then we'll just have to make sure that never happens," Millie said with a determined gleam in her eye. "If someone wants to adopt you, they'll have to take me too, and that's that!"

"Do you mean it?"

"Cross my paws," Millie said, which was her

way of making the most serious of promises.

Daisy relaxed and went back to listening to the pitter-patter of the rain falling on the roof, and the thump of Millie's tail against the floor. She wondered, though, why Danny had touched their heads when he mentioned the event. Millie didn't seem to think that meant anything. But Daisy couldn't help thinking Danny hoped to find new homes for Daisy and Millie, too.

DANNY ROBERTSHAW and **RON DANTA** are horse trainers and animal lovers who began helping dogs way before 2005. But when Hurricane Katrina hit, their rescue began in earnest as they saved over six hundred dogs from that national disaster. For their work during Katrina, they were 2008 ASPCA Honorees of the Year. Since then, Danny and Ron have used their personal home for Danny & Ron's Rescue, formed as a nonprofit 501(c)(3) that has saved over thirteen thousand dogs, all placed in loving homes. Danny, Ron, and their rescue were the subjects of the award-winning documentary *Life in the Doghouse*. They have also been featured on the *Today* show, *CBS Evening News*, the Hallmark Channel, *Pickler & Ben*, and several other TV shows. Their mission is a lifetime promise of love and care to every dog they take in. Visit them @DannyRonsRescue and at DannyRonsRescue.org, and learn more at LifeintheDoghouseMovie.com.

CRYSTAL VELASQUEZ is the author of several books for children, including the

American Girl: Forever Friends series, the graphic novel *Just Princesses*, the Hunters of Chaos series, the Your Life, but . . . series, and four books in the Maya & Miguel series. Her short story "Guillermina" is featured in Edgardo Miranda-Rodriguez's anthology *Ricanstruction: Reminiscing and Rebuilding Puerto Rico*. She holds a BA in creative writing from Penn State University and is a graduate of NYU's Summer Publishing Institute. Currently an editor at Working Partners Ltd., she lives in Flushing, Queens, in New York City and is the go-to dog sitter for all her friends. Visit her website at CrystalVelasquez.com, or follow her at Facebook.com/CrystalVelasquezAuthor or @CrystalVelasquezAuthor on Instagram.

LAURA CATRINELLA is an illustrator and character designer who loves to play with shapes and colors. She has fun creating a variety of different characters and people, all while being able to play around and tell a story with them. Usually, she can be found drawing at a park or coffee shop. Laura resides in British Columbia, Canada, and she spends most (all) of her time with her two mini dachshunds, Peanut and Timmy.